In a little village, on a big hill, there was a white cottage surrounded by trees as far as the eye could see.
A young girl called Amber was visiting her grandad, she was wearing her favourite coat. She always loved visiting Grandad, and always left with happy memories
However, tonight was going to be very … very different

"So what would you like to do tonight?"
Asked grandad Ceril
"A board game, paint or listen to me sing"
Grandad drew a deep breath
"The hills are alive, with the sound of music!" Grandad was a very bad singer, but this made little Amber laugh.
"You're silly, grandad" giggled Amber.
"I would like you to read me a book, can we go sit and read it by the fire"
"And which book would you like?" Grandad replied.

Little amber ran her fingers along the old wooden bookcase, she peered upwards towards a book that was sticking out, but it was too high and she couldn't reach it.
"That one!" She said excitedly
"Are you sure?"
"Yes, that's the one," said Amber.

Grandad, took down the book and went over to a large, brown, worn
leather chair. He sat down and opened the book
Little Amber jumped on his knee.
"What's it about?" asked Amber, pointing to the book
"It's a Christmas story, old but true.
You might not like it If I read it to you" teased Grandad.
"Pleaaaaaase" begged Amber.

"Ok, ok so let the story begin…."

Many many years ago, Santa Claus and the Christmas spirit had a very
important meeting with each other
Santa Claus wanted everyone in the world to be happy, and spend time
with family on Christmas Day.
He wanted everyone, no matter how rich and poor, no matter the
color of their skin to have that one special day.

Where you could eat until your belly was about to burst
Play with the toys that his elves have made
Wear the clothes that grandmas have knitted
And laugh at the jokes that were in the crackers

But the spirit of Christmas wanted balance, he didn't want boys and girls
to be greedy and take Christmas for granted
So Santa and the spirit of Christmas made a deal. They both signed a
contract , and in that contract if the naughty list was ever longer than
the nice list, then all the naughty children would be punished in the
most darkest way…

Everything in the world was going magically, Santa was loved,
people were dressing up as him to show him, love
But on the first of December like every year Santa was checking the
naughty and nice list with Mrs Claus

Mrs Santa was sitting at one end of a long wooden table, her glasses balancing on the end of her nose
On the table were two long lists, with the smallest writing you ever did see

Every minute the names would jump from one list to the other.
This was the naughty and nice list

"SANTA! SANTA! Come quick it's happening" shouted Mrs Claus.
Santa looked at the list, he was shaking and a tear was rolling down
his rosy red cheeks.
"No this can't happen, not after all these years" Santa bellowed
"But it is, "said Mrs Claus",
He will be here anytime soon

In the corner of the room stood a grandfather clock, white and
colorful with the time showing 11:59
Santa and Mrs Claus watched in horror as the seconds ticked by
All the elves and reindeer appeared at the windows looking in
The clock struck midnight. In a poof of smoke emerged in front of
the clock

The spirit of Christmas was a tall man, dressed in a long black leather coat, shiny red boots, and crazy woven hair. He had earrings that were made of Christmas baubles, and in his right hand, he held a rolled-up piece of paper with a black bow.

"Hello, everybody, did you miss me? Do you like my earrings? fancy aren't they! Have you put on weight?" the spirit of Christmas spoke very fast and was excited to be here

I'm sorry, I shouldn't pick on your weight, it's not your fault that you can't say no to another mince pie, you should stop after one hundred.

The Spirit of Christmas let out a belly laugh, Santa Claus was not happy

"Let's get this over with," said Santa
"So you know what will happen, " said the spirit of Christmas

"Yes"

"You sure"

"Yes, I'm not stupid"

The Spirit of Christmas leaned over to Mrs Claus

"Well I do see how you drive the reindeer after too many sherries,
you should seek help!" He whispered, but loud enough for Santa
to hear.

The spirit of Christmas let out another belly laugh

At midnight on the 1st of December, A contract between myself-
the spirit of Christmas- and Santa Claus with Mrs Claus and the elves
as our witnesses:
Any Naughty boy or girl that
Takes Christmas for granted
That doesn't appreciate all the hard work their parents have done to
make Christmas fun
And most of all that isn't kind and generous to those who are less
fortunate.
Will face a terrible punishment.
If they have not changed by sunrise on Christmas morning they will
lose the use of their eyes
The spirit of Christmas smashes down on the frozen contact with his
hammer
The contact breaks into thousands of pieces

"The Christmas spell is cast"
The spirit of Christmas vanishes leaving Santa and Mrs Claus holding each other.
Little Amber lets out a death-churning scream
"Noooooooo grandad noooooo!!!!!!!!"
"Do you want me to stop?" said Grandad
Amber was crying and hugging her grandad,
"Will the naughty boys and girls really not see on Christmas Day?" Said Amber with hesitation in her voice

You see, my little dear girl, not all the boys and girls in the world are as good as you.

They started taking presents and Christmas for granted, they never wrote thank you letters or helped their mum and dad around the house. They just wanted more and more expensive presents each year.

So the spirit of Christmas punished the naughty boys and girls and took away something that everybody takes for granted, the ability to see the wonders of the world.

"But did they get their sight back?" asked Amber

"Every parent in the world had a little magic book, and in this book
was a spell that they could only use twice.
But the spell would only work, if the naughty children did something
nice, if not the child would lose their sight even longer, sometimes a
whole month.
"But what is something nice?" asked Amber.
It could be helping with the Christmas dinner, a hug, or a simple
thank you. It could mean doing something small for a friend or
stranger. But once the gesture had been made the spell was lifted.

So Amber kissed and hugged her grandad, and said the words
"I'm going to make sure no children in the whole world will ever go
blind on Christmas day"
Amber walked out of the cottage, and down the long wooden track.
At the bottom of the track was a row of houses. Amber reached inside
her pockets and took out the spending money she had been saving to
buy a new toy.
She got out a pen and paper and wrote a note to each of the houses
which had children inside. She shared out the money and posted it
through the letterbox.
"May you use this money to treat yourself and others, and always be
grateful for the things you have
Merry Christmas
Amber"

The End.

MERRY CHRISTMAS ONE AND ALL

ILLUSTRATED BY

TAHNEAT SYED

&

AI

Printed in Great Britain
by Amazon

13721936R00016